Lighting the Earth

Written by DIANA LYNNE NADEAU

Illustrated by KAREN NAOMI BROUGH

Aurora Books
Eugene, Oregon, USA

Copyright © 2014 Diana Lynne Nadeau and Karen Naomi Brough

All rights reserved. No part of this book may be reproduced or transmitted in any form or by any means electronic or mechanical including photocopying, recording, or by any information storage and retrieval system without permission in writing from the publisher.

Aurora Books, an imprint of Eco-Justice Press, L.L.C.

Aurora Books
P.O. Box 5409 Eugene, OR 97405
www.ecojusticepress.com

Lighting the Earth
Story by Diana Lynne Nadeau
Illustrated by Karen Naomi Brough

Library of Congress Control Number: 2015919160
ISBN 978-0-9891296-3-3

*With loving gratitude, I dedicate this book
to Sage, Laura, Tina, and Briana.*
–DLN

*For Aiyana and Iain,
follow your hearts and be the Light!*
–KNB

My mama always told me that the most important thing to do is to be a light on Earth. She told me that's why I'm here.

She would always say, "Sashi, you were born to light this beautiful Earth. That's what it's all about, my love. There's nothing else."

I knew what she was saying was important. I didn't really understand it, but that didn't matter. I loved listening to my mama say important things.

Even as I got older, I still didn't really understand. I thought maybe my mama meant I'd have to rope down the sun and hold it. Sometimes I'd stare at the sun trying to figure out if I could find a rope long enough.

One day Mama caught me while I was staring at the sun. "What are you doing blinding yourself like that, Sashi? You're gonna burn your eyes out," she said.

"But Mama, I was trying to find a way to get the sun down here," I told her. "It's so far up and I'm not big enough. I was thinking that if you and Baba helped me, maybe together we could make a really long rope and pull it down. Then I could hold it, and I'd be the best light on Earth!"

"Oh, my stars!" Mama howled. She laughed a belly full, and then she laughed some more. Finally she explained, "The Light I'm telling you about is not just in the sun. It is the Light of all things, Sashi, the very nature of all things, including you."

"Me, Mama?"

"Yes, my dear, but you got to feel the Light, Sashi. You got to feel it in your body, all throughout your body. You got to let it shine from inside you. That's how you do it."

"Am I supposed to become like a flame that's shining then, Mama?" I asked.

"Yes! Sashi, that's it, my love!" My mama's eyes were smiling big. I always loved it when her eyes smiled big like that.

Pretty soon I started to have dreams that I was swallowing bits of light, lots of little bits of light. They were like little balls of fire inside me! I swallowed so many that I kept waking up with bellyaches.

The only thing that made my bellyaches go away was going down to the river and letting the cool water wash me through and through.

But the fire dreams kept coming, so I decided I didn't want to have light in my body. When I told Mama, she didn't laugh. Instead, she looked at me for a long time.

"Sashi," she said tenderly, "let's forget about light for now."

"Okay," I whispered. There was something very calm about her right then, and it made me feel all quiet inside and out. Suddenly I felt really sad, as though there were a heavy weight in my heart. I realized I hadn't figured anything out after all these years.

Mama sat down and gently pulled me onto her lap. Her lap was always warm. It felt like a big hug. She rocked me and started to hum. It was a tune I knew very well. She'd hummed it to me many times before when I was sick, or sad, or angry. Mama called it her 'soul song.'

Then, very softly she asked me, "What do you like to do, Sashi? What is it you like very best of all?"

I sat for a long while, thinking. It was a tough question to answer. It was hard to choose because I liked so many things.

Mama whispered to me, "What is the deepest expression of who you are?" Those were adult words, but I didn't really listen like a kid. Something else in me listened, something very still, something that knew just exactly what she meant.

I suddenly had such a good feeling, I bounced off her lap and shouted, "I like the river very best of all! I love to jump in it! To splash in it! To play in it! To watch the fish swim in it! And Mama, I especially love to just sit nearby and listen to it!"

Mama laughed with joy and clapped her hands. "Yes! Yes, you do, Sashi! And your Light shines so bright when you are with your river!"

"My Light? You can see it?" I asked.

She smiled so big. "Oh, my love, you have such a beautiful, bright Light! And when you are with your river, you become that Light; a light we need so much here on this Earth."

"That's all I have to do? Be with the river?" I asked.

Mama looked me right in the eye, "Be with the river always, and you will shine brighter than fire, brighter than even the sun, Sashi."

I'll never forget how beautiful my mama was as she spoke in that moment.

My Light! I could feel it! It filled me so much that I laughed and hugged Mama all at once. I felt so much love for my mama. She seemed to glow like the sun herself.

I'm bigger now. I spend my days traveling the Earth to protect rivers everywhere. There is no question now, this is exactly how I was meant to Light the Earth. I know in my heart this is why I was born.

And what about my mama? She's still in my village telling kids, "You were born to Light this beautiful Earth. That's what it's all about, my loves. There's nothing else." Now I know this is why *she* was born.

How about you? How will you Light the Earth?

Diana Lynne Nadeau lives in rainy Oregon with her family and two silly cats. She is certified in Conflict Resolution as a Mediator, and has been teaching beginning Tibetan Meditation according to her teacher's instructions since 2012. She loves to swim, hike and camp in the wide Oregon wilderness. Her upcoming picture book entitled, *Tibet, My Country*, is the winner of the 2016 Khyentse Foundation Grant Award.

Karen Naomi Brough lives in the seacoast area of New Hampshire. She enjoys running and hiking with her husband and two teenage kids. Karen loves to read, write, and create art. She is currently working on illustrations for a short story that she has written for young adults.

CPSIA information can be obtained
at www.ICGtesting.com
Printed in the USA
BVOW05s0256030118
504274BV00004B/5/P